COLORING  K

THIS BOOK BELONG TO

....

....

....

....

MW00890662

TEST COLOR PAGE

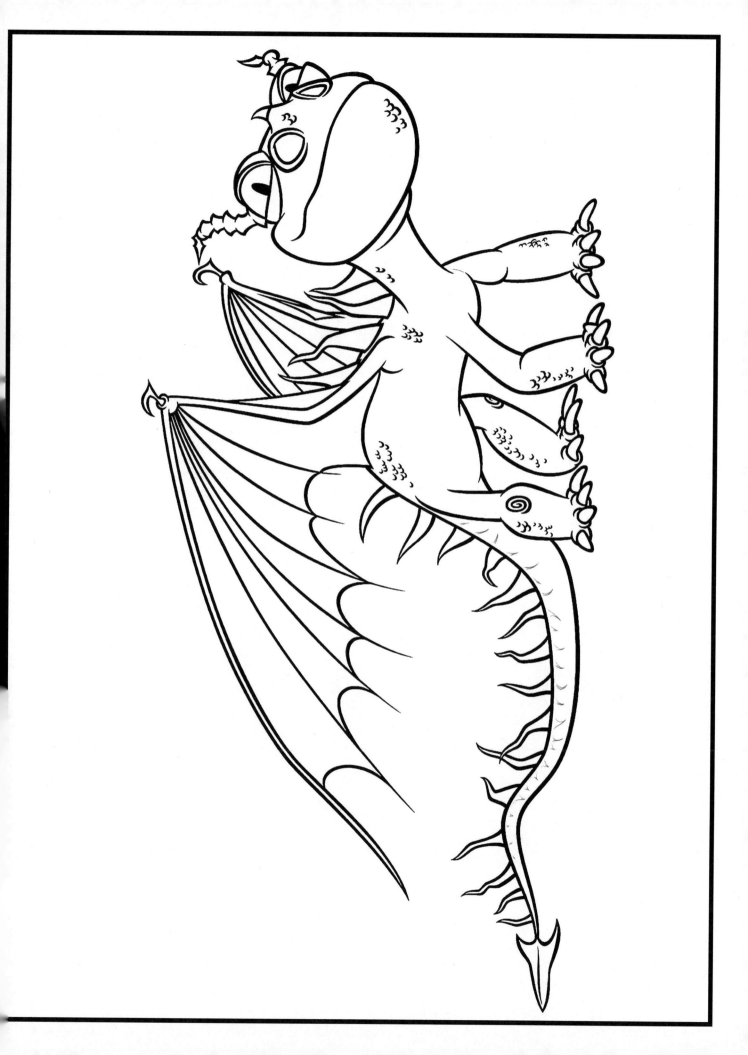

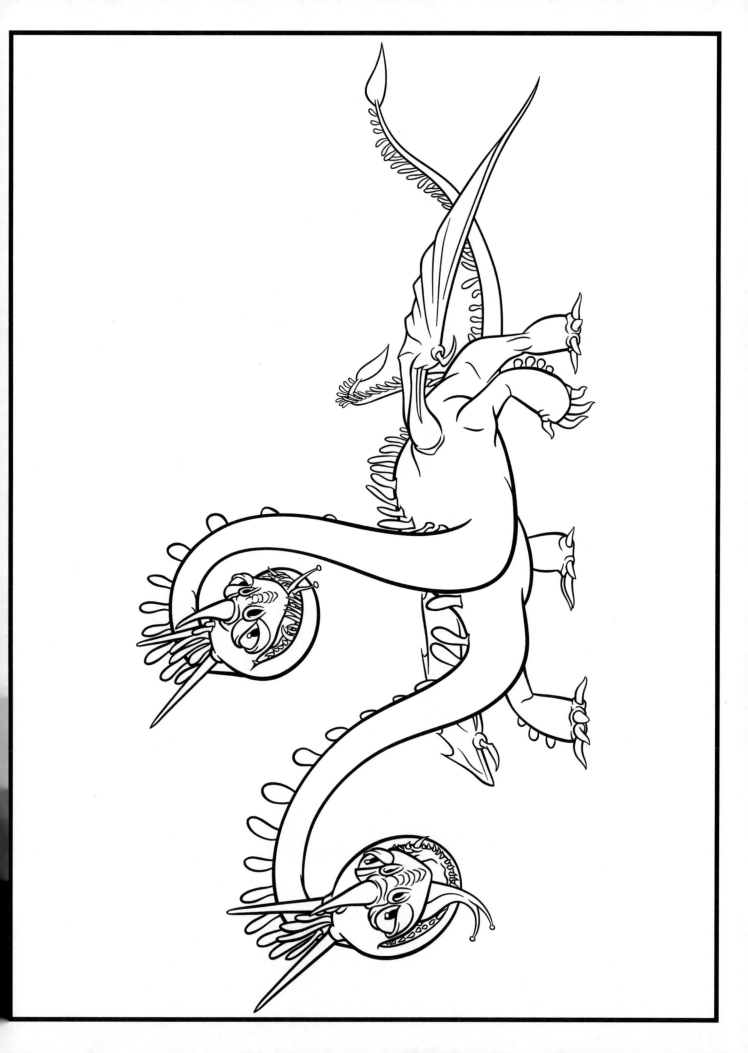

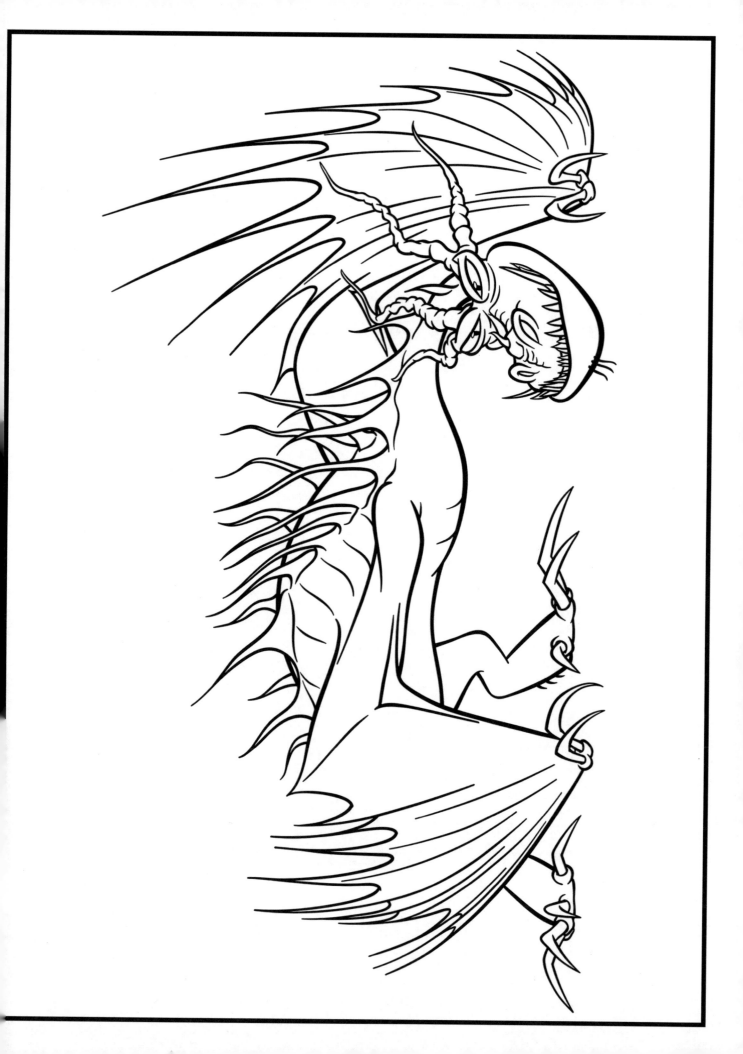

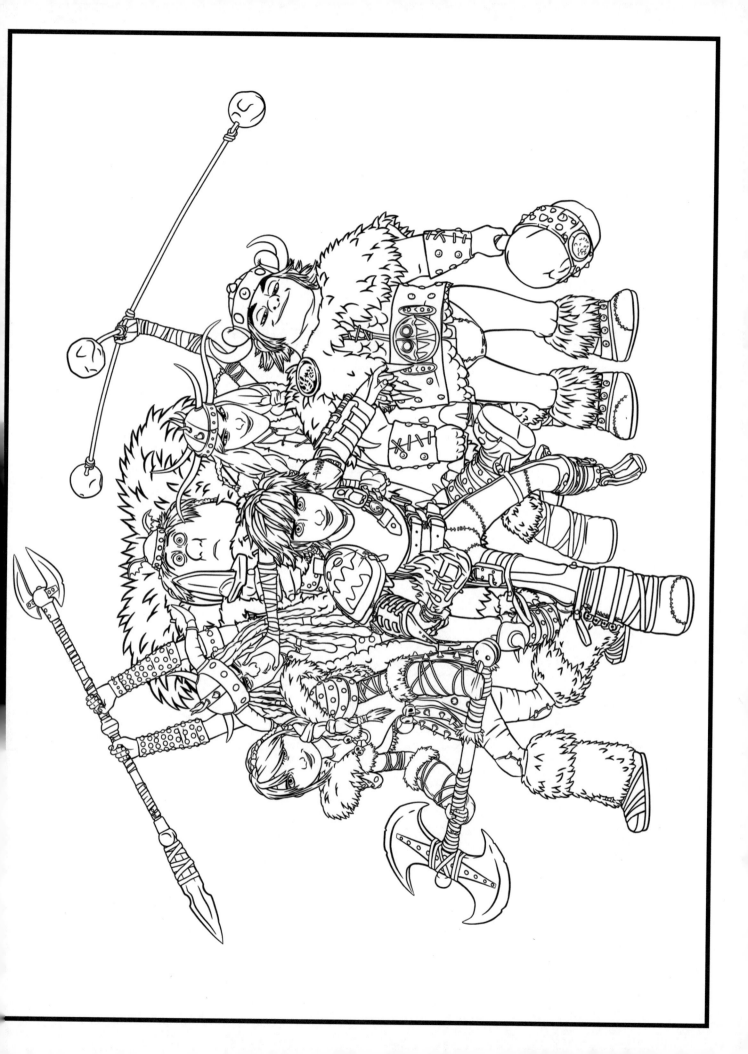

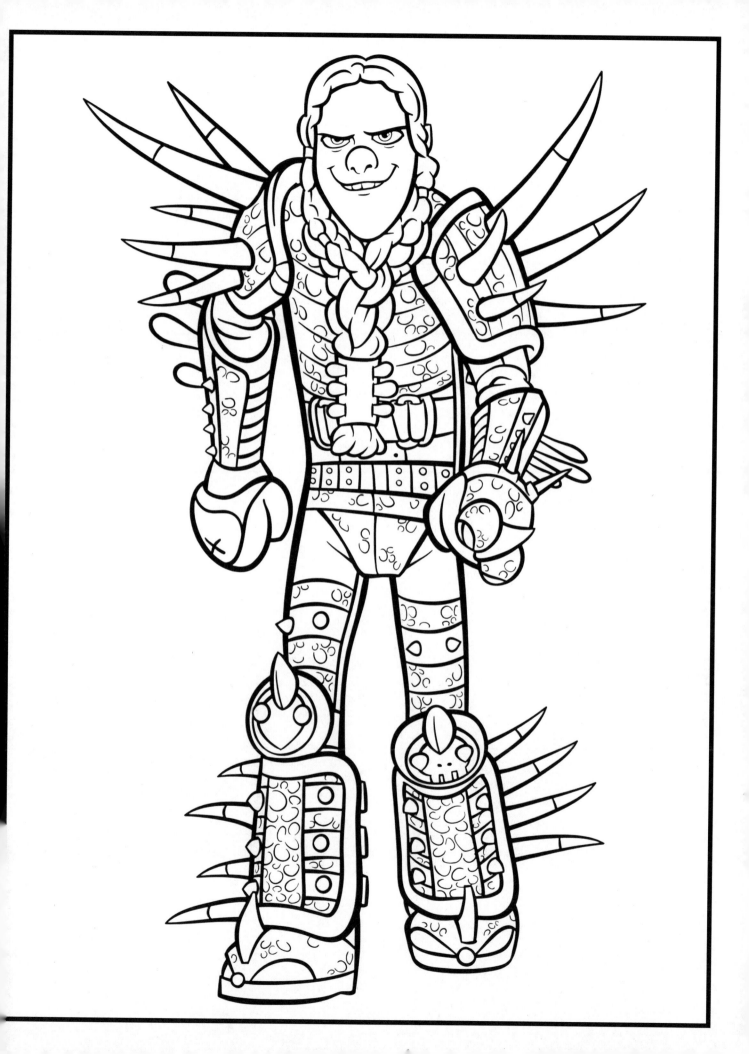

WRITE DOWN
WHAT YOU LIKE ABOUT THIS BOOK:

....

....

....

....

....

....

....

....

....

....

....

....

**THANK YOU VERY MUCH
FOR TRUSTING AND CHOOSING
OUR PRODUCT**

**WISH YOU ALL THE BEST
IN YOUR FUTURE**

**HOPE YOU WILL PUT YOUR TRUST
IN OUR NEXT PRODUCT**